I0539059

An Amendment to Murder

Lawrence Stripling Sr.

Copyright 2016 by Lawrence Stripling Sr.

ALL RIGHTS RESERVED
No part of this publication may be stored or transmitted without the permission in writing from the author and publisher.
This book is a work of fiction. The names, characters, places and incidents are the product of the writer's imagination and are not to be construed as real.

Books-Motion Pictures-Television
Frazier Publishing & Services
P.O. Box 363835
North Las Vegas, NV 89036

TABLE OF CONTENTS

Chapter 1

1989 - CHAUNCEY

Chauncey, an awkward and aloof college student walks into the campus bar. He looks around the place. He doesn't see any of his so called friends. His friends promised to be there forty-five minutes early. He figures they are either late or too afraid to show up. He was depending on their back-up, just in case things turned ugly. He orders a beer, sits at the bar and waits. He is nervous and his hands are shaking. He tries picking up his beer for a sip and it spills down his chin and on to the counter. He looks around hoping no one noticed. Luckily the bar is half empty and the patrons that are there are either playing games, talking or in their own little world. He sees a table by the exit, but it is occupied by a single woman who doesn't look very friendly. He checks the time, quarter to six, he has another thirty minutes until the meet. He calls the bartender over and tells her to send the lady in the corner a basket of chicken tenders and another beer.

. . . .

Kim Norwell is in her senior year. She is making her way through school on money from her Grammy and the Navy reserves. She was a loner with very few friends at the school. In the last four years she may have well been invisible. Tonight she is nursing a beer and eating peanuts. She just spent her last four dollars. The peanuts were just about gone and the beer was warm. She figured it was time to go back to her lonely dorm room.

Kim had a roommate that would drop in, in between boyfriends. The two only tolerated each other and there was no friendship connection there. Kim usually enjoyed the solitude, but tonight she felt as though the dorm room walls were closing in on her. She hoped that a trip to the bar for a beer and people watching would chase her blues away. She noticed a young guy come in the bar. He looked around the room, very nervous like and sat at the bar. He spilled his first sip of beer; it ran down his chin and hit the bar. Kim noticed but turned her head when he looked around to see if anyone saw him.

The bartender smiled as she walked towards Kim's table. Kim was the only one in the corner by the back door. She didn't order any wings. She didn't have any money. But lady stopped at her table, set the wings down along with another beer on her table and said "these are from the man at the bar."

The young guy hoisted his beer and mouthed the words cheers.

Great, Kim thought four years at this school and today was her day to be hit on by a kid barely old enough to drink. She really wanted to be left alone. But on the other hand she was starving. Her choice was, have a conversation with the kid or go back to the dorm. Her stomach betrayer her as it growled at the smell of the tenders. The chicken and beer were too good to pass up. It was time for conversation.

She saw the young man approaching her table. She wanted to send him away, but she already started in on the appetizers that he sent over. She figured he could sit until the food and drinks were done, or the conversation got stale. Besides, the only things in her room were the four walls and an empty fridge. Tenders and fries trump a peanut butter sandwiches and Ramen noodles.

Chauncey introduced himself as he took a seat at Kim's table. Kim shook his hand and thanked him for the food and drinks. Chauncey ordered more beers and began talking a mile a minute. Kim pretended to listen and tried not to make much eye contact. She found Chauncey a bit cocky and self-centered. He reminded her of her younger cousin Marcus.

After the beers took effect, Kim found it was refreshing to meet someone who reminded her of home. She even asked him questions and told him about herself. Chauncey seemed to mellow out after a few beers. He was no longer as nervous as he was at the start. He seemed to drop his guard and Kim figured, maybe he was a good kid after all.

Kim and Chauncey devoured six different appetizers, an entrée and five beers. She was feeling pretty damn good. They were about to order dessert when Kim noticed three guys come into the bar. They were the local guys from the town and not students. There was a short one who seemed to be the leader. The second was medium height and skinny. The third had a little muscle on him, but didn't seem like too much of a threat. She was surprised to see townies on the campus. Usually the only time the townies came on campus was to sell drugs or start trouble.

The skinny guy in the back pointed at their table and made a beeline straight to Chauncey. The one in the middle called Chauncey a few derogatory names. He said he was going to take Chauncey out back and to beat him to death. The third guy sucker punched him in the mouth. Chauncey put his hand to his mouth, saw blood and looked like he was about to cry. The other two lifted him from the chair and proceeded to march him toward the door. None of the other bar patrons lifted a finger to help.

Kim stood up when she saw the leader punch Chauncey in the kidney. She grabbed a beer bottle and hit it on the skinny guy's head. The bottle didn't break like in the movies. She told the men to stop and let him go. The man who had punched Chauncey told her to get the hell out of the way. The man took a swing at Kim. Kim saw it coming and put up the bottle to blocked it. Instead of hitting Kim, the man smacked the bottle out of Kim's hand across the room. It broke as it hit the ground.

What happened next surprised everyone. Kim punched the lead man in the throat, the nose and the stomach. He dropped to one knee gasping for breath. Man number two was on the right of Chauncey. He stepped behind Kim and grabbed her ponytail and yanked her head back. Kim delivered three elbows to his ribs and midsection knocking the wind out of him. He released her ponytail as he doubled over. She then went after man number three. He was to the left of Chauncey. She managed to kick him in the groin with a swift forward kick. She wanted to slow him down, just in case he wanted to join the fight. She turned back to man two. He swung on Kim grazing her left cheek. Instead of stepping back Kim charged the man. She kneed him in the groin and gave him a vicious head butt to the nose. She heard a crunch as blood splattered on his face. He was out of the fight.

Chauncey let out a high pitch scream as the third man wielded a knife toward his throat.

Kim yelled "Get out and run!" as she pushed Chauncey towards the front door. He started to the door, but stopped when he saw the two men ready to attack Kim.

4

The leader was slowly getting to his feet. He threw a chair at Kim's feet, tripping her up and slowing her exit to the door.

In one swift motion Kim grabbed the bar stool and swung it at the leader connecting with his jaw. He fell over a table. Kim turned and swung the chair towards the third man with the knife. He ducked away from the chair and sliced at Kim with the knife. The knife blade slashed the front of her Tee shirt exposing her bra. Kim continued swinging the stool, keeping the man with the knife at bay. She finally made contact with the hand that was holding the knife. The knife dropped at Chauncey's feet. Chauncey kicked the knife toward the bar. The knife owner then punched Chauncey in the face hard, sending him over tables and to the floor. Kim saw an opening. She lunged at the man grabbing his left wrist. She did a quick twist with her body and the wrist snapped. Kim finished him off with a short punch to the temple knocking him unconscious.

The fight seemed to last a long time, but in reality it was only a few minutes. By the time campus security arrived at the bar, the fight was over. Kim had taken out three men with no help from the crowd who watched on cheering for her and laughing at the men on the floor.

Kim reached down and helped Chauncey up from the floor. His face was bruised and battered. He had a swollen eye and a busted lip, but he would be alright.

She looked at her new shirt; it was sliced across the front. There were a few spot of blood. She felt her stomach for cuts, she had been nicked. She looked inside the tear of her shirt and saw it was just a flesh wound. It was nothing a band aid couldn't cover.

The campus police asked questions and spoke to the crowd. The ambulance came and carted the three away. The police sergeant refused to believe that Kim had caused so much carnage by herself. He asked her and Chauncey a few questions before telling them that they were free to go. Chauncey handed their waitress four twenties and the two made their way to the door.

They walked for a while in silence. Chauncey didn't know what to say or do. he never had anyone stand up for him before. He never seen a woman fight like this either. He was amazed.

Chauncey broke the silence "what are you a ninja or super woman?"

Kim smiled and replied "A little bit of both. By the way, who were those guys and why was I defending you?"

Chauncey stopped and looked down at his feet. He was so embarrassed. He took a deep breath and began his confession. "They were the local drug boys from off campus. I deal drugs at the school. Let me be honest, I sell drugs at a cheap price to kids on campus, so that they will let me hang out. The leader Winston the guy with the knife, said that I have been dealing on his turf and cutting into his money. He wanted me to pay him or he would kill me. Last time I paid them off and they left me alone for a while. This time there was no way for me to pay them off. My father refused me an advance on my allowance and my friends were nowhere to be found. I couldn't pay. They would have killed me. That is if you weren't around to save me. Thank you, I owe you big. You saved my life."

Chauncey being thankful bought Kim new shirts, pants and meals for the remainder of the year.

Chapter 2

ADAIR

The day Chauncey's father showed up at Kim's dorm was a total surprise. Kim was running late for class as usual. She was in disarray. She had a pop tart in her mouth, a jacket slung over her shoulder and books under her arm. She had two minutes to get to class. She yanked open the door to the hallway and ran right into a very well-dressed older man who stood ready to knock. Kim being all of five foot six inches and half the size of the man, fell back on her butt dropping everything including her pop tart on to the floor.

The big man reached down and helped her up. The man asked "Are you Kim, Kim Norwell?"

Kim was looking down at her pop tart and replied "yes sir, that's me." When she looked up the man had a smirk on his face. He stared at her funny and laughed.

He asked "You're telling me that you are Kim Norwell?"

Kim was now a little pissed as she said "yeah, I am Kim Norwell, do you have a problem with that?"

The big man backed down quickly. He stuttered "No, no problem, I just thought, well you know that you would be bigger. Let me introduce myself, I am Adair, Chauncey's father."

Kim stepped back noticing a slight resemblance. She said "Nice to meet you Mr. Adair. What can I do for you?" With the heavy Spanish accent, he pronounced his name like (au the air). She held out her hand for a shake.

He said "Please, just call me Adair. You saved my son's life." He pushed her hand to the side and embraced her in a big bear hug." He then held onto her shoulders and moved her backwards to arm's length. He stared at her like she was a puppy or a toddler."

He looked at her seriously and said "So you beat up three men and saved my boys life? You must be one tough little cookie. I guess looks can be deceiving. You are so tiny and so cute."

Kim smiled. She knew she was tough. Since the day of the fight Kim went back to business as usual. The kids around campus were talking and she was even asked for an interview in the school paper. She declined. Now, it just dawned on her what she had done, she beat down three men in a bar. She suddenly felt a wave of dizziness come over her. She closed her eyes and let it pass. She didn't think at all during the fight. Once the adrenaline kicked it, she was in a zone.

Kim asked Adair into her cramped dorm room. Adair sat on the tiny chair that went to the desk. Kim sat on the bottom bunk. They shared pop tarts and drank milk as he spoke.

He said he was there to offer Kim a job. He was very vague about what the job entailed. He mentioned exterminating and high profile people. Kim thought to herself, was Adair offering her a job to kill people? He mentioned the job would be challenging and something he was sure she would enjoy, not mentioning that it paid well.

He handed her a black glossy card with just a gold embossed phone number on it. He said think about it, when you are ready, call me anytime. You will always have a job waiting for you. All you have to do is call that number and say you want the job and it is yours

Kim didn't show much interest in the job. At the time she thought whatever the man was up to, she didn't want any part of it. It all sounded like the mafia. Kim thanked Adair for the job offer as she walked him to the door.

He asked what her plans after college were. She smiled and told him of her plans to serve as a Marine, kill people around the globe and one day retire to a cushy job in the Pentagon.

He smiled and said the job he was offering gave her the same opportunities. He told her that if the Marines didn't work out to give him a call, he could put her talents to good use.

Adair left the room. Kim looked at the card once more, turning it over in her hand, wondering what that was all about. She looked down by the door noticing an envelope. She picked it up. She thought maybe Adair had dropped it, until she noticed her name neatly written on the front. Stapled to the envelope was another black glossy business card like the one she held in her hand.

The envelope had a little weight. She opened the envelope and slid the contents onto the desk. It was money. Lots of money! More than she had ever seen. There were fifties, twenties and tens. She counted Five thousand dollars' total. She ran out into the hallway, but there was no sign of Adair. She counted the money again and sat on the floor laughing out loud, wondering what the hell just happened.

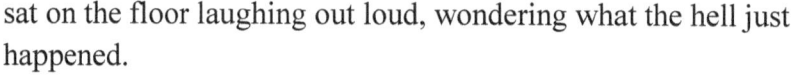

After college Kim did three years in the Marines before being put out on a general discharge for insubordination. She had trouble with authority.

During her time in the Marines, she became a marksman, sniper and a few other things that if she mentioned, she would have to kill you. She loved the Marines, but hated being told what to do. Although she was an officer, she was still under someone else's command.

Kim and Chauncey had stayed in contact during the time that Kim was in the Marines. Chauncey was now working for his father. He constantly mentioned to Kim that if she wanted a new career, the job his father had offered was still hers.

Kim finally asked Chauncey if his father was a mobster. Chauncey laughed and told her no. He explained how his father was on the other end of the spectrum from being a mobster. Adair is a good guy, going after bad people. Chauncey told Kim all about his father and explained what he could about the secret society he referred to as the Committee.

Kim liked what she was hearing. She could be the hit woman that she always dreamed of as a child. She told Chauncey that she would consider the job and be in touch. In reality, she had already decided to take the job and call his father as soon as she got off the phone with him.

Kim called the number on the black shiny card. The phone rang once and Adair answered "Hello, how may I help you."

Even though it had been three years, Kim remembered the voice. She said "Hello Adair, this is Kim Norwell, how are you doing? You may not remember me, but I am a friend of your son Chauncey." She hesitated, not sure if he would remember her or not.

He quickly answered "Hello Kim, I am so happy that you called. Are you ready to accept my job offer? It would be a pleasure to have you on my staff."

Kim laughed and said "Well Adair, you just made me an offer that I can't refuse. It would be my pleasure to join your staff."

Adair said "In that case Kim, Welcome to the Committee. We will be contacting you soon. Have a good day." He hung before she could thank him or say goodbye.

Kim dialed her childhood friend Rodney. When he answered, she yelled into the phone excitedly "I'M GOING TO BE A HIT WOMAN!"

Chapter 3

PRESENT DAY

Kim Norwell looked at her caller ID and quickly answered the phone. "Hey sweetie, how are you doing?" It was her business partner and childhood friend Rodney Price.

"Hey Kim, I'm doing well. You sound a little rushed; did I catch you at a bad time?"

Kim sighed then chuckled. "No, I have a moment. Believe it or not, I'm waiting for a Mr. Wright to come into my sight so I can exterminate him."

Rodney asked "I thought you were in surveillance mode on the dude for a few more weeks?"

"That was the plan, but apparently Mr. Wright has signed, sealed and delivered an early death warrant. Seems this idiot was caught with his hand in the cookie jar. He was helping himself to company funds for a number of years to the tune of two million dollars. Then to add insult to injury, he was fishing off the company pier and managed to catch himself an office intern. Problem was the intern was the twenty-two-year-old step daughter of one of the partners. Sounds like Mr. Wright can do no right."

Rodney whistled and said "Wow, sounds like that brother has problems."

"Well, those rich folks and their petty non-sense are the least of his problems. Rodney, I got a call at five AM this morning telling me that my fee has been doubled if I can take this guy out today. Five AM Rodney, there is no five AM on my clock. My day starts at ten. Then you know how I hate driving in rush hour traffic. Forty-five minutes of gridlock traffic, on a motorcycle is crazy. Now I'm lying on the ground waiting for this idiot to leave for work so I can exterminate him. Oh and today of all days he decides to be late for work. What a day this is turning out to be. I should shoot him in the balls just on principal alone."

Rodney let out a gasp and said. "They woke you up at five in the morning and made you drive to the city. Damn, this man has got to die!"

Kim laughed a sweet laugh. "Thanks partner. Mr. Wright is lucky it's not that time of the month or else I would go Rambo on his ass. You know how I get when I'm craving chocolate and my tubes hurt. No one in this city would be safe."

Kim's tone quickly changed from cheery to serious as she spoke in a very calm voice. "Rodney can you please hold the line; I see my friend coming out now."

Nothing was said for a few moments. Rodney heard Kim slowly inhaling through her nose and exhaling through her mouth. Then quiet, almost as if the line went dead. Rodney sat waiting, practically holding his breath. He pictured Kim taking aim. She lined the man up in her rifle scope crosshairs, ready to take her shot. He heard Kim mumbling a few curse words under her breath.

Kim spoke to herself. "That's it darling keep coming. A little more sweetie, that's it, right there." Rodney held his breath as he waited for the shots. Pop! Pop! Pop! Three muffled shots came in quick succession. The shots startled him as he sat frozen holding the line. Knowing Kim was a hit woman was one thing, but actually hearing her take the shots that would end a life was suddenly unsettling.

Kim was back on the line. "Hey Rodney, are you still there?" She sounded pretty chipper for someone who just took a life.

Rodney took a moment to answer. "Yes, I'm here." He felt as though he croaked the words. His throat was dry and his palms were moist. His heart was now racing a mile a minute. He felt as though he had been sitting right next to Kim as she pulled the trigger. He fought the urge to yell into the phone. He wanted to tell his friend to get out of the city as fast as she could. But the words wouldn't come. He could hear her dismantling the rifle, closing the gun case and running toward the stairwell. Rodney could tell by her labored breathing and the slight echo that she making her way down a stairwell. He heard a door opening and then city traffic. He assumed she made it safely to the street. He breathed a sigh of relief.

Kim asked in a rushed voice. "How about we meet for lunch in an hour?" She put a finger to her earpiece and adjusted the volume. She mounted her motorcycle and adjusted the guitar case on her back. The guitar case was modified to hold the long barrel rifle.

14

She casually started the engine and waited for her friend's reply, nothing.

She was now in mid-morning traffic making her way to the bridge. Traffic was light and moving smoothly. She was passing over Eighth Avenue headed to ninth. There were now ten blocks between her and the apartment building where she took her shot. More than twelve blocks between her and the man who she shot in the heart three times.

She sensed quiet over the phone. She could feel that Rodney was shaken. What the hell was she thinking, answering the phone during a job. It was dangerous for her and she knew better. She could have been distracted and missed the shot. It was bad for Rodney. Him hearing the gunshots was like putting him on the scene. She hit herself on the head twice with the palm of her hand.

Kim blinked back tears and asked quietly. "Baby, are you alright?"

Rodney shaken from his thoughts managed a simple reply. "Unh huh, I'll be fine."

Kim said softly. "Cool, I'll see you at Myron's in an hour, love you." She hit the disconnect button on the earpiece. She thought about how she and Rodney met after every hit. It was Rodney's idea. He would always start by saying that he was there for her. If she chose to talk, that was fine, if not, then that was cool too. Today Kim felt that she may need to talk. To tell Rodney what it was like to kill and how she could kill so easily with no remorse.

She pushed a tear away. What the hell is happening? This was the second time this morning that she felt a cry coming on. She told herself that she would have a good cry later that evening. She would open a bottle of wine and a box of chocolates and let the flood gate flow. She laughed at the thought of crying. She shook her head, gunned the engine and took to the open highway.

Chapter 4

RODNEY AND KIM

Rodney and Kim were seated outdoors on the deck of Myron's. Myron's was a sports bar of sorts with a limited menu. Salad, soups and a few appetizers lined the left side of the menu. The right side of the menu featured drinks, desserts and a few entrees. The chicken choices were baked tenders or wings lightly sauced or naked. The three burger choices were grain fed Kobe beef, farm raised turkey or a garden vegetable. The featured seafood choices were salmon and the catch of the day. The dessert choices were fresh baked oatmeal chocolate chip cookies, key lime pie or carrot cake.

At this time of day Myron's was practically empty. The staff was cleaning up after the lunch rush and beginning preparations for the dinner crowd. Kim and Rodney usually met at this time for a quiet uninterrupted conversation between old friends.

Rodney watched his friend devour the decent sized meal. He always wondered how she could stay so fit and eat so much. Kim wasn't one for salads and veggies. She didn't have an intense exercise program. She wasn't a calorie counter and she never met a dessert that she didn't like. At forty-five-years-old, she could easily be mistaken for a woman in her mid-thirties. He shook his head and smiled. What a beautiful and amazing woman.

Kim felt Rodney's gaze upon her. She looked up from her meal to see him staring. She had mayo on her chin and barbecue sauce on the corners of her mouth. She simply smiled and asked him "what, is there something in my teeth?"

Kim occasionally caught Rodney checking her out. It was usually during the times when she was checking him out. He was so strong, very handsome and always focused. He ate healthy, exercised regularly and had the willpower to resist sweets. Since their first meeting over thirty years ago, Rodney treated her with respect and was always there for her. Always just a phone call away. In her eyes, he was the sweetest and most amazing man alive.

Rodney took his napkin and carefully wiped the mess from her face. Looking at her, he asked "How do you do it?"

"Do what?" she asked innocently. She had a feeling where this conversation might be headed.

Rodney asked "You execute someone in the morning and in the afternoon, you carry on as if nothing happened. Doesn't it bother you?"

Kim studied her friend carefully. She took a long drink of her strawberry lemonade. She had pondered those very questions in her own mind for years and never had a good explanation. At this moment nothing new seemed to materialize.

18

Kim cleared her throat and began to speak. "Rodney, earlier today on the phone, you heard the shots. I shouldn't have answered the call. I know what I do must seem crazy to you, but it's just a job, a job that I am actually good at it and I like."

She paused then continued speaking. "The people I exterminate are bad people. Most have made a mockery out of the justice system. Others have gotten away with murder. The rest are on someone's list to be taken out for Lord knows what reasons. When I get the call I know that someone has made up their mind to have someone exterminated. If I don't do it, then they will hire the next guy or girl in line. There aren't many women in this line of work. That make it a plus for me. I can get in and out of places undetected. Let me ask you, what do you think of when someone says it was a hired hit?"

Rodney paused, thought for a moment and said "Usually a white guy in a fancy suit and expensive car or a crazed white dude on a building with a high powered rifle. I guess that is what the movies have us to believe."

Kim smile and agreed "exactly, so for me to walk in, make a hit and walk out unsuspected or unnoticed, is a huge rush. Being a hit woman is comparable to a typical nine to five job. You work it while you are there and come the end of the day, you leave it behind until the next working day. Except with a nine to five, you have to continue working with people you would like to kill. She sensed that Rodney somehow understood.

Rodney laughed and said "great analogy." He reached over and held Kim's hand. His look said that he didn't judge. The simple nod and his smile said he did understand.

Kim continued by telling him that she didn't kill women, children or the elderly. You have to draw the line somewhere. She said it was satisfying taking bad people off of the streets. She told him that outside of her business associates, he was the only person who knew what she did for a living.

Rodney said "I'm glad that you laid it out on the table for me. It all makes good sense." He sat in silence for a moment then asked "Did you save room for dessert? Want to share a slice of carrot cake."

Kim smiled and said "A man after my own heart. Let's do the key lime pie instead." Kim relaxed in her seat and unbuttoned the top button on her jeans. She let out a quiet burp and said "on second thought, let's get a slice of both."

After sharing a slice of key lime pie and a slice of carrot cake they decided it was a good idea to walk off the desserts. They strolled through town talking and window shopping as they made their way to the river to watch the sunset. Perfect ending to a somewhat crazy day.

Chapter 5

LESTER

Kim was livid as she screamed at her friend Chauncey, on the other end of the phone. "I didn't say that I have a problem exterminating two people. I don't have a problem with exterminating a congressman. Chauncey you know I do not exterminate women. How many times have I told you that I don't hurt women or children? In case you hadn't noticed this Lester person happens to be a woman. When I saw the name Lester, I thought it was a man. When I think of Lester, I think of a man. Don't you think of a man when you hear the name Lester? For Christ sake Chauncey, what kind of parent would name their daughter Lester? What kind of woman would go through life being called Lester? Help me out here Chauncey, I really don't think I can exterminate this woman."

"There is nothing that I can do Kim. I told you that I tried talking to the Committee and they refused to discuss it. They reminded me that when you accepted the contract you gave them your word that you would carry out the job. I don't see the problem. Just think of her as a man, with breast. It sounds like an easy kill. Quick in and out, we will set it all up for you. The woman is bad news and a loner, no one will ever miss or care that she is gone." Chauncey tried his best to make her feel better about the hit, but was having very little luck.

Kim took a calming breath. She rubbed the bridge of her nose and spoke quietly into the phone. "The Committee knows that I don't exterminate women. I told them that when I signed on years ago. I have an agreement with the Committee; under no circumstance would I exterminate a woman or a child. Chauncey, please explain to me why they would give me this hit? This is bullshit and I do not like this one bit. You have to get me out of this, please Chauncey. I am begging you."

"Sorry babe, there is nothing I can do. When you signed on with the Committee, you agreed to take out whoever they chose. No questions asked and no exceptions. There is no way that you can back out of this hit now. You know as well as I do that if you don't go through with this hit, the next name on the Committee's list will be yours." Chauncey explained once more.

"Dude, there must be something we can do." Kim was now pleading. Her reply came out barely above a whisper.

"I'll call you back in an hour. I'll see if there is anything I can do. In the meantime, If I were you, I wouldn't get my hopes up." With that said Chauncey hung up.

Kim searched for the phone that she received by messenger service, two days earlier. Each assigned hit was sent by text on a burner phone. Kim was reviewing the encoded text message to make sure she deciphered the details of the hit correctly. She decoded the words again, making sure that she had the name right. She did and there was no mistake, the name was Lester.

She re-read her encoded text reply that said she accepted the hit. This was her electronic signature and her word. She would have to honor the contract. She whispered to herself softly. "Damn it, what did I get myself into."

Chapter 6

CHAUNCEY – THE MIDDLEMAN

The Committee consists of a group of executives, police, politicians, judges and lawyers. They exist to serve justice for the public on their terms. Their task is to review a person or persons whose name comes before them. This person has either committed a heinous crime or what they feel are insurmountable crimes against society. The Committee decides the guilty person or person's fate. The members have two choices, let the taxpayers send them through the revolving door we call the Judicial system or take them out of the system, permanently. The vote must be unanimous for the Committee to take action and set the ball in motion. The Committee is the judge and jury. Chauncey is the broker or middleman. Kim is the executioner.

Once Kim receives information on a hit from Chauncey; she is given a twenty-four-hour window to decide if she wishes to take the hit or pass it along. She usually goes over the package with her childhood friend Rodney Price. Rodney does some detective checks to see if the Committee has a legitimate reason for executing a hit. Rodney tells Kim whether or not he agrees with the recommendation and leaves the choice up to her. If Kim agrees then she lets Chauncey know that she accepts the hit. Chauncey lets the committee know Kim's decision. Within hours a cell phone is sent to Kim. A text comes shortly after containing a vague contract. When she replies her agreement, the contract is final. A sizable amount of small unmarked bills is delivered discreetly by carrier to Kim's front door. The deal is done and Kim soon makes the hit. Kim has yet to refuse a contract. So far, she has completed every job cleanly. Meaning nothing will ever point back to the committee. If she messes up, she is on her own.

Kim knows very little about the committee and found it best not to know or to ask. The

Information she receives comes directly from the middleman Chauncey. He informs her of a job through a phone call or encrypted text. He passes along a little inside information to help her decide if she wants the job or not. He does upfront legwork to make sure the job can be done and Kim will come out of it safely. He secures the area and supplies everything she needs for a hit.

As a middleman Chauncey is going well above and beyond the normal job description. A middleman or broker usually makes the call and collects his money. No additional information is passed. No help is rendered. Just the phone call was needed to seal the deal. Chauncey on the other hand has been at every one of Kim's hits, hidden just beyond the shadows.

Unbeknownst to Kim, Chauncey harbors deep feelings for her. Actually he is madly in love with her. He often wonders why she can't see it? Why can't she love him the way that he loves her? He wished that just once, she would look at him the way she looks at her friend Rodney Price.

Chauncey has hung out with Rodney and Kim many times over the years. Rodney is a tall guy, about six feet five inches. He towers over Chauncey by a good nine inches. He is also a solid, muscular guy making Chauncey seem tiny by comparison. Chauncey has tried many times over the years to not like Rodney, but just couldn't bring himself to do so. Rodney is a decent guy who has always treated him with respect. He calls Chauncey little brother and makes him feel as such. Chauncey gets the feeling that if anyone ever picked with him that Rodney would have his back. The same way Kim did the first time she saved his life.

Chapter 7

KIM

Rodney was talking to Kim on the phone. He was asking whether or not she decided to go through with the hit on the woman named Lester. She was just about to answer when her phone beeped. It was Chauncey on the other line. She told Rodney that she would have to call him back.

Chauncey paused for a second before he said "Bad news Kim, I can't get you out of this one. It has gone through committee and they are expecting it to be done. You will have to see this one through. Dad says that the ball is rolling and you have the usual time plus an additional seventy-two hours to close the deal. Sorry I couldn't do anything to get you out of this"

Kim asked "Alright then, tell me what she did that was so terrible and let's see if it will change the way I feel. Come on, work with me on this man" After a few deep breaths and a long massaged the bridge of her nose she began to calm. Her head ached as though someone inside was pounding a crazy jungle beat.

Chauncey whined "Come on Kim, give me a break. You know that I am not allowed to tell you specifics of a hit. I can only tell you the who and the where but not the why. You know how it goes. I get a call. I make a call. I am only the messenger. Besides, I have no information on the people who are sentenced to death. It's plain to see that this lady Lester Carson must be into some serious shit to have her name come up on the Committee's list. Listen Kim, you are a hired killer that is what you do. Look at it as just another job"

Chauncey chuckled into the phone and said "I never knew a contract killer with a conscience or such high morals"

Kim managed a smile, then shook her head and said "I have a conscience that surfaces from time to time and I am a lady, so most days I have morals. Listen I know it's just a job, but until I got the package, I thought this Lester dude was a man. You know someone who deserves to die. The kind of scum that would chop up a poor schmuck for kicks or knee cap a hardworking man because he owed his boss a few thousand dollars. Maybe kill an innocent family to get back at a rival. But man, for it to be a woman named Lester, it's throwing me for a loop"

Chauncey now sounding concerned asked "So, Kim, can I hold you to your word and trust that you will honor this contract?"

Kim paused for a beat, then answered "Yes, of course I'll honor the contract and make the hit, I gave my word, didn't I? I will just have to do a little improvisation and a lot of thinking on the fly, that's all"

"That's my girl" Chauncey said with a sigh of relief.

Kim released a loud sigh into the phone. She then took a deep breath and counted to ten and released. She said "Chauncey, I know I'm being a jerk. Really, I'm sorry, you don't deserve this. You are just doing your job and being a good friend. You're right, murder is murder and a contract is a contract. There are no rules to killing. Either I'm going to exterminate a person or I'm not. It's what I'm paid to do. But I don't know man, this is so different, how do I justify killing a woman"

Chauncey asked. "I'm curious? If this has you so torn, then how do you justify killing men?"

Kim laughed "That's easy, all men are assholes. My daddy and granddaddy were assholes. When I look at men, I see assholes. When I get a hit on a man, I know that that bastard did somebody wrong, somewhere and he deserves to die. Every time I get one of you bastards in my sights, I scream "this one's for my daddy, you bastard!" Kim laughed louder. "Face it Chauncey, all men are dogs. Either they did dirt, doing dirt or about to do dirt"

"I'm sensing serious daddy issues and possibly a little penis envy going on here" Chauncey was now laughing. He was happy that he was able to lighten the mood.

"Yeah, I have big time daddy issues. Penis issues, not so much. I like my vagina too much and the power that it has over men and …..."

Chauncey cut Kim short, "I just thought of something. Why not add an amendment to murder? Let's say if a woman commits a heinous crime against another woman or takes the life of a child. Then your amendment to murder would give you the right to kill with no regrets."

Kim asked seriously "So, are you saying if a woman kill other women or a child, it is pretty much open season on that woman? Are you telling me this Lester chick killed a woman or child?"

Chauncey was on the verge of giving up said "If it would make you feel better about killing this Lester chick, then yes, we'll say that she stalks and kills women, babies, puppies, Bambi, thumper and Winnie the Pooh, damn. Kim, please go kill this woman already."

Kim smiled to herself. As crazy as it sounded, Chauncey had a point. As an unwritten rule in the contract killing business, women and children are usually off limits. Unless it is one heinous deed they performed. Lester Carson must have done something really bad for the committee to want her dead.

Kim's conversation with Chauncey begins to wind down. They go over the things she will need for the hit. He assures her that everything she asked for will be delivered a mile from the hit location. He repeats the list; A nondescript Honda civic four doors, dark gray or black, tinted windows and two .38 short pistols with silencers in the glove box.

Chauncey leaves Kim with a few words of advice. "Lose whatever conscience you think you have and go terminate this freaking woman. It's just a job and she's just a mark. Best of luck. Call me after the hit and we'll do lunch." The line goes dead and Kim is left staring at the phone.

Chapter 8

RODNEY, LESTER & CONCLUSION

Kim listens half-heartedly as Rodney talked about his full time accounting job, his part time detective agency and the chief of police passing on another cold case for him to investigate. The tequila he was drinking had loosened him up a bit. She noticed that Rodney was slouching a little in his seat and he didn't mention a word about her being late.

Kim was pushing her food around the plate as she listened. Taking an occasional nibble, she would nod, smile and say an occasional "um hum" or "wow" to show interest in what Rodney was saying.

"What's up Kim, you seem distracted?" Rodney asked as he buttered another roll.

Kim fidgeted and calmly asked "Really, why do you say that?"

Rodney replied "because I asked you what your plans were for the weekend and you answered 'yes, that was nice.' Spill it, what has got you so shook up?"

Kim tried to avoid his question, but he had the look that said there was no way she was getting off the hook. So she gave in "Well Rodney, I would like your feedback on a few things that have me torn." She played with the spoon in her coffee, looking up occasionally.

"I'm all ears, let's hear it." Rodney pushed his empty plate and shot glasses to the middle of the table. He wiped his mouth, then sat back in his chair and gave her his undivided attention.

"Well, first off, I have been contracted to exterminate of a person by the name of Lester.

Rodney laughed "Lester? What possible crime to humanity could a man named Lester commit. When I think of the name Lester, I think of the ventriloquist and his dummy Tyler. Lester and Tyler I think that was their names. What happened did Lester kill his dummy Tyler?" Kim could tell that the few shot of tequila had Rodney on the edge of drunkenness. Any other time he would have been dead serious.

Correcting Rodney, Kim said "It's Willie Tyler and Lester. Lester was the dummy."

Rodney said "So Lester is the dummy? That means that I don't know of any man named Lester or Tyler for that matter."

Kim touched Rodney's arm and said "Honey, Lester is a woman."

Rodney laughed harder "A woman named Lester? Boy, her parents must have wanted a boy something fierce to name a girl

Lester. This is like that song "A boy named Sue." Instead of killing Ms. Lester, you should go after her parents for naming her Lester."

Kim gave Rodney a stern look and said "You know how I feel about exterminating women and …."

Rodney politely raised his hand like a kid in school finally getting Kim's attention.

Kim sighed "yes Rodney?"

He said "first of all you kill people for a living, you don't exterminate them. You exterminate rodents and roaches, not people. I mean seriously, can you just say kill? Say it with me, I kill people for a living" Rodney chuckled, obviously enjoying his tormenting.

"Dammit Rodney, get serious. I know what I do, you don't have to remind me."

"Then why can't you just say kill?"

"I don't actually kill people. I rid the world of those who exploit the system. I rid the world of human waste. I exterminate them.

"I got it, you don't kill, you exterminate and rid the world of human waste, and I stand corrected. The world is forever in your debt. Thank you." Rodney conceded. He bowed his head in a respective manner and put his hand together as though praying and sat quietly.

Kim smiled at her friend. He was tipsy, but not drunk. This was the perfect time for her to get information on Olestra "Lester" Collins. Rodney had his laptop and as a detective he could get information from sources that she couldn't access.

He sat relaxed in the corner of the booth with his legs out stretched on the seat. He had finished two baskets of rolls, a ten-ounce sirloin, large sweet potato and veggies. Kim decided one more shot couldn't hurt, so she flagged down the waitress and ordered a shot for Rodney and one for her.

"Mr. Detective, now that you are feeling no pain, I need you to dig up all the dirt you can find on Ms. Lester Collins and her congressman friend. I don't have a first name for the congressman, but what Chauncey tells me, he is a real piece of work. Something about this hit just isn't sitting right with me. I am regretting taking this hit.

Rodney took a sip of tequila sucked on a lime and licked salt off the back of his hand. Kim had seen Rodney do this so many times before. Drinking expensive tequila always loosened him up.

Rodney flipped open his laptop and typed furiously. He read for a while and let out a quick whistle. He typed more as he spoke. "I remember these two. These two have been known to cause chaos and leave bodies in their wake. They just aren't just bad; they are Michael Jackson bad." Rodney laughed at his own joke.

Kim asked "Why are they bad, what have they done?"

Rodney said "I came across these two a year or so ago while investigating the Bond family. You remember old man Bond, the old moonshiner and flesh peddler that lives up on the hill. Rumor has it that these two were on payroll for years. The politician was bought and paid for and your friend Olestra "praying mantis" Collins, was known to lure men into bed and bite their heads off. Not literally bite their heads off, but lure men of power into bed and blackmail them. She could make or break men from here to Washington. All she had to do was leak a few photos and careers would come crashing down or skyrocket to the moon. Depending on who paid the most money. Usually she played both sides against the middle and the only winner was her."

"Do you mean she was in the Bond Cartel? That is one bad ass cartel; someone I wouldn't want to mess with?" Kim had a look of fear on her face

Rodney laughed and said "Lies, all lies. Yes, the Bond's at one time were notorious moonshiners during prohibition. Everybody who is anybody bought their booze from them. They also were flesh peddlers; you know big into prostitution. Their motto was sex, moonshine and the swing in the thirties. Rodney laughed, you know, like sex, drugs and rock and roll in the sixties. Anyway, the old man was out to show everyone a good time, at his expense. The Bonds made butt loads of money and didn't pay one cent in taxes. The reason being is that they owned people. They owned politicians up and down the eastern seaboard. They owned state and local law officials. They had bribed anyone who would take a dollar. These people weren't dangerous; they were just generous to a fault. In other words, they gave away most of their fortunes making that sure everyone stayed drunk, happy and under the covers, in more ways than one if you get my drift. This way authorities were going after the other guy and leaving them alone. The reason they weren't caught running moonshine is because no one was looking for them. If someone turned them in or tried to prosecute, then the skeletons would mysteriously start falling out of the closet. It seemed that old man Bond had the dirt on everyone.

The old men Bond era cartel as you call them have gotten old and live in seclusion or have passed on. The people they had the goods on are either out of power, dead or in jail. So the Bonds are no longer a threat.

The new Bond family, or as I call them, the Bond 2.0 have a net worth is in the billions. Bond 2.0 invested their inheritances from the elder Bonds and distributed their wealth amongst the children and grandchildren. Giving each a fair share of stocks, bonds, land holdings and legit businesses throughout Tennessee and along the eastern seaboard"

"If the elder Bonds were doing so well, why would they give up on the extortion game. It sounds like such a lucrative venture. I mean they could always buy the new politicians" Kim asked puzzled.

"The elder Bond's, who folks believed were ruthless killers, were just old fashioned people with old fashioned ideas. They believed in an eye for an eye. You know, kill my dog and I'll slay your cat. That kind of thing. They could be vicious when crossed. Sort of like you." Again Rodney laughed at his own joke. But like I said earlier, they supplied the party to everyone who wanted a good time. Now days everyone parties behind closed doors or online. The original Bonds are extinct dinosaurs.

"The children and Grandchildren on the other hand are Ivy league educated and computer savvy. The children and Grandchildren are living very well on family money. The problem is the Grandkids are all very promiscuous. Seems the present generation are recreational druggies who live for the party. The party gene had skipped a generation. What they don't snort up their nose or shoot in their veins, is invested in huge money making ventures that give them even more money to shoot in their veins or sniff up their nose. Are you with me on this?" Rodney took another drink and slowly returned to his relaxed position.

Kim asked "So what does congressman and the Lester woman has to do with the Bonds and their money?"

Rodney smiled and said "Just getting to that sweetheart. The congressman comes from a long line of politicians. Each of his family members were politicians living on Bond money. The Bonds financed their campaign and kept them in office. That was until Carla Bond came along. Carla Bond the eldest of the grandchildren. This lady is all business. When she speaks the family listens. She has told the family to dump the congressman and send him on his merry way. She closed the pocket book and now she is trying successfully to ruin him. In return your congressman has found the closet that holds the skeletons to a lot of people's political careers. He has made a lot of enemies of politicians from here to Washington and they want him dead."

Now, to the lady that you know as Lester is otherwise known as Olestra Collins.

Kim asked "Is that name supposed to mean something to me?"

Rodney snorted "Maybe, if you were part of high society and the country club elite. My sources tell me that your friend Lester was all about the dollar bill. She would do just about anything or anybody for money. Rumor has it that she was the side piece of Carla Bond."

Kim started to see where Rodney was going with this. She asked "so what you are telling me is that Lester is in bed with the congressman and the woman who is trying to destroy him?"

Rodney looked up from the computer and said "Looks like it. People in the high society circles are shying away from Lester because of what she may know from pillow talk with the senator. Plus, the volumes of pillow talk that she may have of her own. For years she was said to be sleeping with the husbands and wives of the rich and famous, so just imagine the stories this woman could tell"

Kim looked at her friend and said "I am killing because of some high society bullshit?"

Rodney looked at her and said "Not quite, in all of the society shenanigans it seems that Lester and the congressman have been very bad over the years. I mentioned earlier about leaving bodies in their wake. Seems that Lester convinced Carla and some of old man Bonds friends to invest millions on land deals that the congressman said would make them rich, excuse me, richer. Turns out the congressman and Lester were selling other people's land, government owned property and estates of deceased people. People that they made deceased, get my drift?" They were killing people and selling their land. Catch my drift?"

Kim asked "So, Carla wants them both dead for the double cross?"

Rodney thought and said "No, from what I hear, Carla is not a killer. I doubt that she would have her lover or the congressman killed over money, not when she is making millions a day. Anyway it sounds like Carla and Lester's relationship was no secret. My guess is that Carla has other lovers on the side as well. The woman is gorgeous and can buy and sell anyone she wanted. From what I am reading here is your duos have stepped on the toes of county, state and government officials and Lord know who else. They were one step ahead of everyone, until now. Everyone has seemed to have caught up. So anyone one of these groups could have paid you to exterminate their man and girl"

Rodney was now talking in his mellow tequila voice. He was staring with a goofy grin on his face. This meant that he was really buzzed and teetering on sleep. Kim was a little tired herself and had to let what he told me sink in. That was a lot of information. Kim had the waitress put her dinner in a doggy bag. The Steak and mashed potatoes she would eat for breakfast. The ice cream dessert she would eat as soon as she was snug in her bed and in front of the television. Kim ordered a coffee for Rodney and espresso for me. She slid over to Rodney's side of the booth. He held her in his arms as they talked about traveling, vacations, beaches and sunsets until the waitress came to tell them the bistro was closing.

LESTER

The dinner with Rodney was very informative and Kim still had reservations about killing the woman, but for the most part she would go through with it.

Kim arrived in Lester's neighborhood driving an indiscreet Honda Civic, silver with tinted windows. She set her escape routes and then decided the best way to handle the job. She rarely did break-ins due to so many unknowns. There were pets, nosy neighbors, and a bystander noticing a car that didn't belong in the neighborhood and looked suspicious. It was standing out for being the lone black woman in an all-white neighborhood.

She was riding down the street when a pedestrian walked out from in between two cars with not so much looking before they stepped into the path of her car. Kim swerved quickly into the oncoming lane, luckily there was no traffic. She didn't honk her horn as not to bring attention to herself. She looked in her rear view mirror and noticed as the pedestrian continued to make his way across the street oblivious as to what just happened.

During Kim's trial run of the neighborhood a few days earlier, she noticed that it was a somewhat upper class community. It is located just inside the inner city limits, a few blocks from downtown. Street traffic was brisk during the day and very light in the evening. The neighborhood was made up of mostly singles, mostly white with the occasional interracial couples mixed in. This was the type of neighborhood where neighbors prided themselves on living in harmony, whilst making sure they didn't invade each other's personal space. Not the type of neighborhood where you would ask to borrow a cup of sugar, a garden tool or stand on the front lawn having an hour long conversation with Fred or Bob. This was a modern day condo community where all exterior work was governed by the association. An exorbitant monthly condo fee covered everything to do with the exterior. This meant that no one would be out doing yard work this evening. Kim was feeling a little better about this job. She would possibly fit in and not stand out too much. The only problem would be getting inside the house.

Kim parked the Honda at the end of the block. She steps out looks around and heads for the corner. She wanted to make it look as though she had been there before and knew exactly where she was going, so no hesitation. She turns left and passes the first set of condos. Each one looking like the other, only difference is the color of the door or maybe a flower pot on the stoop. There is an opening between the units that she takes. She turns right and makes her way to the back yards. Each condo has a privacy fence six feet high. The fence is on the right, garages on the left.

She feels a vibration in her left pocket, she looks at the message from Chauncey, it reads "Back fence is open, use left French door. They are both upstairs, looks like you are about to interrupt their love making, you may want to let them finish." Kim looks around but can't tell where Chauncey is watching from. She texts back "thank you for the recon, I owe you big. Stop watching them getting busy, you pervert." The last text from Chauncey said "best of luck, see you at dinner."

Kim makes her way to the third unit and looks through the slats in the fence. There is a small outdoor Jacuzzi that is still steamy, but not on. The French door is slightly ajar, one door open, the other secure. Kim tries the back gate, it is open. She makes her way around the Jacuzzi to the back door. She pulls out a thirty-eight and puts a silencer in place. She steps into the darkness and allows her eyes to adjust. She sees the glow coming from the upstairs. She knows the layout, bathroom at the top of the stairs, bedroom first door to the left, smaller bedroom for guest or storage and at the end of the hall, a master suite with personal bathroom.

Kim makes her way slowly up to the top of the steps and waits patiently. She hears the last of their love making. She figures that between the two empty bottles of wine on the patio and the round of sex, the two should be very well tired.

Kim, with gun in hand, eases to the edge of the bedroom door and peeks in. She watches as the lady, Lester rolls off the far side of the bed and makes her way to the bathroom and pulls the door closed, but it doesn't fully engage. The congressman is laying on his back, partially covered in a sheet, snoring loudly and facing away from Kim, perfect she says to herself. Kim listens for Lester. She hears the water run, then vigorous tooth brushing.

Making her way to the bed swiftly, Kim grabs a pillow, lays it on the man's face and shoots two quick rounds into his skull. The man's body rises abruptly, and then goes limp. The snoring ends abruptly. She reached down with a latex gloved hand and feels for a pulse, no pulse. She then points the gun toward the door, Lester is now gargling and humming quietly.

That was easy, one down, one to go.

Kim makes her way to the bathroom and listens intently. Lester has just flushed the toilet and there is a splashing water noise followed by what sounds like a hand dryer. Kim wonders what was going on behind the door. Does this lady have a blade? She waits behind the door thinking that Lester would return to the bedroom. Instead, she hears more humming and water falling from the bathtub faucet.

Kim makes her way to the bathroom door and peeks in. Lester is singing loudly as she fills the tub.

Lester yells out "baby, will you be joining me?"

Kim nudged the door open just enough to look in the mirror. In the mirror she sees Lester sitting totally nude on the edge of the tub with her back to the door. Kim pushed the open and says "Baby won't be joining us today."

Lester turned seductively and smiled. She looked Kim up and down and slowly raised her hands. She said "hey gorgeous, you won't be needing the gun, as you can see, I am unarmed. Why don't you get yourself a drink and join me?"

Kim said "sorry Olestra, this isn't that type of party." Holding the gun steady on her Kim said "Seems like you and your friend out there have been very naughty and someone wants you both to very dead."

Kim enters the bathroom and leans against the door jam. She takes the room in. The bathroom is very large and spacious. A lot larger than Kim would have imagined. She figures the master bathroom must be a combination of the original master bath and a third bedroom.

The light gray and emerald green color scheme was refreshing. The artwork was fantastic and the vases were filled with beautiful fresh cut flowers. The gray green speckled countertops were made of real granite, not like the imitation stuff that adorned Kim's bathroom.

The toilet and sinks were the touch-less type with water saving devices. Kim looked past the toilet and notice a French base in the corner. She always wondered what it would be like to have a squirt of water on your private parts after a quick pee. This bade even had a dryer on top, so you didn't even have to wipe yourself dry. This was too cool; her friend Rodney would never believe this bathroom. She would have to get a picture of this bathroom before she left. That would be after she took a pee, used the base and dried her private parts of course.

Kim finished her look around the bathroom and then focused her attention back on Lester. The woman was now sitting on the edge of the tub brushing her long curly blond hair. She was singing again. Kim stands at the door arms crossed with gun in her hand. Kim thinks she should kill her just to stop the singing, it is horrible.

The lady is true blond and the hair is real, no extensions. Her body is slender, long and lean, but slowly giving way to age. She has a slight protrude to the tummy and a hint of love handles. She is very tanned all over. Not the type of tan you get from the salon, but the type you get from hours on a nude beach in the Caribbean.

Kim studied Lester's reflection in the full length mirror that filled the wall behind the tub. Her face was make up free. She must have scrubbed her face before brushing her teeth. Kim noticed four make up removing pads in the trash can. Her face was beautiful despite showing worry lines. She had high cheekbones like a model and thin lips that turned down at the corners. Kim figured her age as late-thirties, but her looks told a different story. This life has aged her a few additional years.

Lester finally looked up into the full length mirror and caught sight of Kim watching her. Their eyes met and locked. Neither of the women blinked, neither one said a word. Lester turned to face Kim and noticed the gun was now on the counter.

Kim said "Sweetie, please don't scream and no sudden moves, OK." Kim raised her hands slightly off the counter, letting the gun sit on the counter. "I am a little unsure of what to do here, so let's have a little girl talk for a moment, OK." Kim said patiently with a softness to her voice that Surprised her.

"Who are you and where is my man?" Lester asked stonily, looking more suspicious than scared.

"Honey, my name is Kim and, well your man won't be joining us tonight. He had a little accident"

"Accident, what accident, he was just in the bed asleep, what did you do to him?" Lester said with very little concern in her voice. "Did you kill him?"

"Well, it seems that dude crossed paths with the wrong people and they figured it was in their best interest that he should cease to exist. So they called me and here I am, in your bathroom. Which is awesome I might add, did you do this all yourself? You have great taste"

A slight smile of pride crossed Lester's thin lips. She looked around the bathroom as if it were the first time seeing it. "Thank you and yes, I did the bathroom and the rest of the place by myself. Glad you like it." She looked at Kim, and then cleared her throat, what she said next surprised Kim. "Can I see him? I want to make sure that he is really dead"

Kim sat on the counter for a moment taken aback, not sure what to say or do. She stood and slowly tucked her pistol in her belt at the small of her back. She took the robe from the back of the door, checked it for weapons and when she was satisfied that there were none, she handed the robe to Lester without saying a word.

Lester took the robe and put it on without closing the front. She took a deep cleansing breath and said "let go."

Lester led and Kim followed. They stopped at the edge of the bed. Lester looked down at the lump in the covers. The man's hairy chest was exposed and the pillow with two bullet holes covered the head. "Are you sure he's dead?" Lester asked staring at the body.

"You can take a look under the pillows if you'd like. I wouldn't advise it though. I used .38 hollow points, they go in small, but make a nasty exit wound. To answer your question, yes he is very dead and won't be coming back to life anytime soon." Kim said

"God, I wish I could have mustered up the nerve to shoot the bastard myself. So many times I thought of killing him, but just couldn't go through with it. I even bought a gun, took the lessons and everything. When it came down to it, I chickened out. He beat me, treated me like shit and had me do things that I am not proud. Kim, I hated this mother fucker with a passion, but through it all, I could never find it in me to kill another human being. I'm a lot of things, Kim, but a killer, I am not" Lester looked to Kim and said "no offense."

Kim said "None taken" Kim was smiling inside. She was starting to like Lester. The woman was very strong in her own right. She didn't scream when she saw Kim standing in her bathroom with the gun. She didn't Freak when Kim told her that she had killed the congressman and she remained unfazed when she saw the body. Apparently this was not her first time seeing a murdered person. Kim was thinking that maybe she didn't kill, but not to be naïve, the woman has had people killed.

Lester opened her mouth and a tiny voice spoke "Kim, I know we just met and all, but can I ask you a favor? Can I shoot him a few times for all of the hell that he has put me through, it would make me feel better?"

Kim thought about this for a moment and said "I can do that, if you agree to do me a favor in return"

Lester agreed "Anything you want." She was getting a good vibe from Kim. Even though they just met, Lester felt like if they would have met at another time, they could have been good friends.

Kim said "I will let you shoot him. You just have to promise not to do anything stupid, like try to shoot me or I will have to shoot you where you stand."

Kim smiled at Lester as the solution to her problem popped into her head. Murder suicide, Kim thought to herself, I could stage a murder suicide. That way she wouldn't have to actually kill Lester, Lester would kill herself. This would be an amendment to murder, just like Chauncey had mentioned.

Kim asked nicely "Do you keep your Valiums and sleep aids in the night stand or the bathroom?"

Lester answered "Bathroom"

Kim touched her elbow and said "Cool, let's go" Kim nodded towards the bathroom. Lester led the way.

Back in the bathroom Kim looks in the medicine cabinet and sees a ton of medicines. She finds Valium, Quaalude and a good variety of sleep aids. "Damn girl you must have a lot on your mind to need this many pills to put your ass to sleep." Kim dumps a small variety of pills on the counter and tells Lester to pick her poison. Lester picks two Valium tablets and a five other pills in various bright colors. "This should take the edge off." Kim returned to the bedroom and grabbed a bottle of vodka and a tall glass from the night stand.

Kim said "Here drink this to knock them back with." She handed Lester the glass filled with vodka.

Lester eyes the glass and says politely "Thank you, if I didn't know better, I would say that you want me to kill myself?"

Kim says to Lester "You're welcome" not answering her question or making eye contact. "Please, have a seat." Lester puts down the toilet seat cover and sits. Kim continues "We are going to work a few things out here. First, you are going to write a suicide note." The blond is handed a pencil and a pad of paper." You will write, I fucked up, I fucked up bad this time or something of that nature. Then, second, we are going to make our way to the other room, so you can have a few shots at dude like I promised"

Lester spoke quietly. She is visibly shaken. "You know something funny; I thought about suicide for a long time, I just couldn't bring myself to do it."

Kim chuckled softly and said "I should shoot you for your terrible singing and screwing such a god ugly man. But I'm not going to kill you. You are going to kill yourself because I don't kill women" Kim smiles warmly, looks her in her tear filled eyes and says "Honey you all fucked up and by the looks of it, you and your boyfriend fucked up bad this time. Trust me, if I don't kill you, they will send other people to kill you and they won't be so nice. I don't want to know, nor do I need to know what you all did. I just

48

have a job to do and it is only half done. Hear take a pill and wash it down with vodka. This will help you put an end to all of your problems."

Lester does as she was told. She opens her mouth to speak, at first nothing comes out, then she finds her voice. "You know, I wanted to get out of this mess long ago. She was talking as she swallowed the pills followed by a swig of vodka. The money just wasn't worth it anymore and I felt like a cheap whore, I hated myself. I know you don't care and you are only here to do a job, but I deserve to die for what I have been doing, I should have known better than this. You don't know how many times I thought of killing myself, but just couldn't do it. These men were paying me well, but passed me around like a cheap whore and I did everything for them, but kill …... "

Kim interrupted, "Hey now, I told you, no personal shit, and no telling me what you did, deal? Apparently it had to be some messed up shit, or else I wouldn't be here. Do you understand me? Are you feeling pretty good now?"

Lester was now laughing and slurring. She said "Good enough to shoot a mo fo in the face"

Kim helped her to her feet and told her "Well, I already shot him in the face, why don't you do a couple of body shots. I'm going to walk you to the bedroom. Try anything and I will shoot you understand"

"Yes ma'am."

Lester does as she was told. She stands over the body, she was expecting to see a bloody mess, but all she saw was the old man's body with a pillow over his face. She asked "Not much blood is it?"

Kim quietly says "There is blood, but it is all in the mattress. Now, what I am going to do is put my gun in your hand and you will shoot him in the chest OK? If you do anything stupid like try to shoot me, I will kill you slowly and painfully understand?"

Lester reached for the gun with her right hand and Kim quickly pulled it back and said "no, you are lefty, I saw you writing."

Lester chuckled and said "Yep, I'm a lefty, sorry, I was just in a hurry to shoot."

Kim secured the gun in Lester's left hand and told her, "I know you've shot a gun before and I believe that you know what to do. Both hands on the gun and squeeze the trigger slowly." Kim stood behind Lester as she steadied for the shot.

Lester replied calmly "OK"

Kim pulled the comforter up to the congressman's neck. Kim walked Lester forward to within three feet of the body, stood next to her and said "you are going to shoot once to his chest. That is all. I took out the rest of the bullets. So one shot, go"

Lester took aim and pulled the trigger, as the bullet hit the body, it rose off the bed. Lester shouted at the man, "You fucking bastard" and pulled the trigger three more times before handing the gun to Kim. She slowly turned and made her way back to the bathroom.

Kim asked "Do you feel better"

Lester slurred "Yes, I do and thank you, that felt awesome. I wanted to do that for a long time.

The drugs were obviously taking effect. Kim walked Lester to the side of the tub, removed her robe and helped her to get into the massive tub. Kim handed her a few more pills and had her drink the vodka until it was gone. Kim sat by the tub, watching the pills take their lethal effect.

Kim sat on the floor not really sure what to do now. Did she push her head under the water and drown her? Did she wait for her to drift off from the drugs, hoping that she goes peaceful and not in a fit of vomiting?

Lester put her hand out and motioned for Kim to come close and take her hand. Kim sat beside the tub and held Lester's hand.

The music in the background seemed too coincided with the mood. Stevie Wonder Tuesday Heartbreak played as both women listened intently, letting the music take them away.

Lester was now bearing her soul. She spoke of a childhood taken away too soon by a sexually abusive father. Her mother's an alcoholic and drug abuser. Her being a throw away child, shuffled from one family member to another.

Kim felt like a priest hearing the woman's last rites.

Lester had stopped crying. She sighed and in an exhausted voice said "I love you and I want to thank you, Kim, you are an angel. No one has done this much for me. I am so tired, I am going to sleep now, bye-bye"

"Goodbye Lester and the thanks is all mine, sleep well my friend."

Lester slowly fell into a deep sleep as Kim watched. Kim thought, what a beautiful girl, what a waste of a life. Kim knew that no matter how she felt, this woman was just as bad as the men she served. Kim was happy she could end this young troubled life in this way. Lester was now passed out, overdosed and slipping slowly into the tub. First her mouth went under then her nose. She gave a violent jerk as her head submerged into the water and the last breath of life left her body. She was at peace now.

Kim stood, looked at the toilet, not having to or wanting to use it. She left the suicide note on the sink, removed the silencer from the gun and tossed the gun into the bath water. The gun was untraceable and only had Lester's prints on them.

Kim said a prayer for Lester's soul and walked through the bedroom, not looking back. She made her way through the house, turning off lights and turning up the air conditioner to full blast. This would delay the stench of the bodies for a few days. She knew that someone on the congressman's staff knew he was here and when he didn't show for a few days they would come for him. As for Lester, she was a loner and made it through this world on her own.

Letting herself out the back door, the same way she came in, Kim locked up the house and made her way through the wood privacy fence. She walked leisurely to the Honda as it sat at the end of the block. She got behind the wheel, started the engine and turned on the radio. They were playing a song from Patti Austin called summer is the coldest time of year. She turned the car around and drove slowly past Lester's condo, looking up at the windows. It was so dark, so cold and lonely. Lester didn't have any true friends or associates. She had no one to look out for her and no one to care for her.

Kim made her way to the highway feeling melancholy. A tear ran down her cheek as she sang along with Earth Wind and Fire's song burning bush. She thought that song was too sad a song for the moment, so she turned the radio off and drove in silence.

She picked up the phone and called her good friend Rodney. He answered on the first ring. In between laughing and crying Kim managed to say "Rodney, honey, I made the hit and I didn't have to exterminate a woman. I will call you later. I love you." They said their goodbyes and disconnected.

CONCLUSION

For the next three days Kim searched every electronic media and paper print newspaper trying to find out what happened to Olestra "Lester" Collins and the congressman. She wondered how the powers that be would cover it up.

On the fourth day, there it was on the front page in bold print "Congressman from Tennessee dies in one car crash"

The article went on to say. The congressman was returning from a fishing trip at his favorite secluded fishing spot in the Land between the Lakes area located in the western part of the state. He had been away for an extended weekend with long time Army friends that he fought alongside in Viet Nam. The Congressman, a second Lieutenant in the war was traveling through a deserted region east of Lake Cumberland when he slid off the road on a rain slick road and went down the side of a ravine. Friends said that when they called to see if he made it home from the three-hour drive there was no answer on his cell phone and his wife said that she hadn't heard from him in the past five hours.

The congressman's friends met at Lake Cumberland and followed the path that he said he would take home. Police searched cell towers for his last connection. A short time later, they saw the skid marks and tire tracks that led to the edge of the cliff. They immediately called county rescue. Helicopters were flown in and searched throughout the night. At daybreak the car and body were recovered from a creek. The remains were positively identified as the Congressman from Tennessee.

A small private service will be held at his home and burial will be in his family's cemetery plot in his hometown.

Kim frantically searched the articles looking for any mention of Olestra Collins or her possible suicide. There was nothing.

She slowly closed her laptop. Words could not explain her devastation. She was stunned.

She forgot that Rodney and Chauncey were sitting across the table from her. Almost in unison they asked "are you alright?"

"Cover up, a freaking cover-up." Kim said too quietly to herself.

Chauncey spoke first startling Kim. "Looks like you did ole girl a favor"

Rodney shook his head and made his way across the table to give Kim a comforting hug. He looked sternly at Chauncey and said "Lighten up man, give her a break.

....

The next day Kim found a paragraph on the police blotter and ambulance run. It reported an account of Olestra Collins death.

Police and rescue teams were sent to the address of Olestra "Lester" Collins in the early hour of the morning. Ms. Collins was found in her condominium by a friend. Her friend mentioned that Olestra had not returned her calls for a few days. When police and paramedics arrived on the scene, a woman's body was found in the bathtub. The body had been in the tub for a few days. Sleeping pills and alcohol were found next to the tub, but autopsies show there were only trace amounts of the pills and an alcohol level of .02 in the system. Not enough to be fatal. The death was ruled as an accidental drowning by the county coroner. No forced entry, no signs of foul play.

The END

Frazier Publishing thanks you very much for your support.

www.ingramcontent.com/pod-product-compliance
Lightning Source LLC
Chambersburg PA
CBHW020651130626
46552CB00003B/1505